For two little dogs who inspired me:
Winnie (who loves hats) and
Lenny the Brave (who is now running in the
fields that will never fade) —love, S.L-J.

For Katie, Ben, and George —D.L.

Text copyright © 2019 by Sally Lloyd-Jones
Jacket art and interior illustrations copyright © 2019 by David Litchfield

All rights reserved. Published in the United States by Schwartz & Wade Books, an imprint of
Random House Children's Books, a division of Penguin Random House LLC, New York.

Schwartz & Wade Books and the colophon are trademarks of Penguin Random House LLC.

Visit us on the Web! rhcbooks.com

Educators and librarians, for a variety of teaching tools, visit us at RHTeachersLibrarians.com

Library of Congress Cataloging-in-Publication Data is available upon request.
ISBN 978-0-399-55815-3 (trade)
ISBN 978-0-399-55816-0 (glb)
ISBN 978-0-399-55817-7 (ebook)

The text of this book is set in Kepler Std.
The illustrations were rendered in mixed media, including pen and ink, watercolor, and Photoshop.
Book design by Rachael Cole

MANUFACTURED IN CHINA
2 4 6 8 10 9 7 5 3 1
First Edition

HATS OFF to MR. POCKLES!

WRITTEN BY **Sally Lloyd-Jones** ILLUSTRATED BY **David Litchfield**

schwartz & wade books · new york

For Mr. Pockles, going without a hat was as unthinkable as going around without any pants on.

an Eating Cornflakes Hat

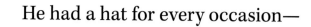

He had a hat for every occasion—

a Having A Little Sit-Down Hat

a Drinking Cups Of Tea Hat

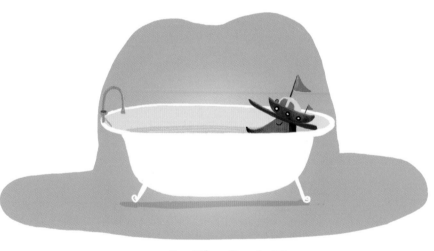

an In The Bath Hat

a Going To Bed Hat.

His only sadness was that he couldn't wear all of them at once.

(There was one hat he NEVER wore because it was

Too Special and he was saving it for Best.)

Maybe it was because he was too busy with his hats to go out and meet people. Or maybe it was because he was terribly shy. But whatever the reason, poor Mr. Pockles had no friends. Sometimes he was a little lonesome.

But then he only had to think of his millions of hats . . . and pop one on. "It's funny how wearing a hat cheers a personage up," said Mr. Pockles.

Until one morning, when it didn't.

It was Hat Day at the PandaPolitan Club, and Mr. Pockles desperately wanted to go and show off all his hats. But only pandas were allowed. And pandas, as everyone knows, are very Black-and-White. Either you are a panda, or you are not.

So, to cheer himself up, Mr. Pockles decided to go
to Treat House instead, to buy himself a bun.

"I shall wear my Jaunty Hat With A Friendly
Feather," he said, thoughtfully.

To his delight, when he got there, Mr. Pockles found it was Bun of the Month Day. (The buns this month were Tasty-Licious Fluffy Fudge Bonnets.)

As he was waiting in line for his Bun of the Month, who should walk in but a panda.

"IT IS I, LADY COCO FITZ-TULIP!" she announced as she sailed to the front of the line. (Lady Fitz-Tulip was a fourth-generation San Francisco Panda and Very Important and even had streets named after her.) She was wearing the most unusual hat Mr. Pockles had ever seen. He couldn't stop staring at it. "I'm late for Hat Day at the PandaPolitan Club!" she cried, waving an invitation around. "I MUST start my spring in style!"

The shop went silent. Everyone felt depressed. They wanted to start *their* spring in style, too. But they didn't have any hats. And they weren't pandas.

Meanwhile, certain baby bunnies (who'd been waiting in line A Long Time and were awfully hungry) mistook Lady Fitz-Tulip's hat for the Bun of the Month and started eating it.

Before anyone realized, they'd eaten the bananas, the grapes, were halfway through the pineapple, and had started on the chopsticks.

"MY ANCESTRAL HAT!" Lady Fitz-Tulip screamed. "Help! Help!" It was too late. The Ancestral Hat fell to the floor. Demolished.

The baby bunnies leaped off the hat
and vanished under their mother's skirt.

"Whatever shall I do NOW?" Lady Fitz-Tulip wailed. "It's HAT Day, and I don't have a single—" She crumpled into a heap.

Everyone rushed around. They picked up her bag. They sat her down. Mr. Pockles even gave her his bun.

"Most kind," said Lady Fitz-Tulip. "Thank you, sir."

"You're most welcome, madame," said Mr. Pockles.

"My aunt made hats, you see," she explained through a mouthful of bun.

"OH! How LOVELY!" said Mr. Pockles.

"But they were all lost in the earthquake . . ."

"OH! How HORRIBLE!" said Mr. Pockles.

"And now I don't have a single hat!" And she began loud sobbing again.

Everyone hung their heads.

Mr. Pockles blinked. It was quite the most awful story he'd ever heard.

But then! Mr. Pockles jumped up. "IT IS I, MR. POCKLES!"

he announced. "Lady Fitz-Tulip, we haven't a moment to lose!

HOLD ON TO YOUR HATS, EVERYONE!"

And even though they didn't have any hats to hold on to, there was nothing to do but follow Lady Fitz-Tulip and Mr. Pockles . . . all the way to Hat House.

Mr. Pockles ran straight upstairs. "Dear Lady Fitz-Tulip," he said, opening a hatbox. "This is . . ."

It was his Special Hat.

It was so beautiful it made all the air go out of the room.

He put it on her head. And showed it to her in a mirror.

"OH!" she gasped. "Mr. Pockles!" And before Mr. Pockles knew what was happening, Lady Fitz-Tulip picked him up and hugged him.

She turned to the door. "We haven't a moment to lose!" She
dropped Mr. Pockles. "HOLD ON TO YOUR HATS, EVERYONE!"

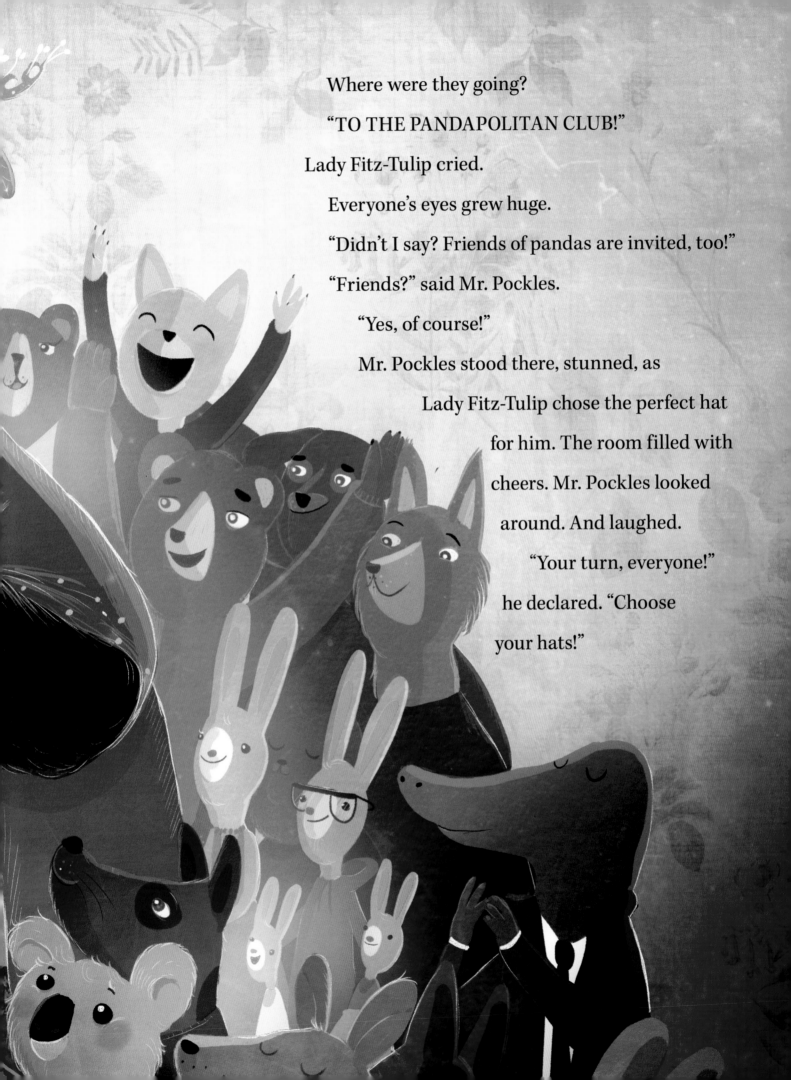

Where were they going?

"TO THE PANDAPOLITAN CLUB!"

Lady Fitz-Tulip cried.

Everyone's eyes grew huge.

"Didn't I say? Friends of pandas are invited, too!"

"Friends?" said Mr. Pockles.

"Yes, of course!"

Mr. Pockles stood there, stunned, as

Lady Fitz-Tulip chose the perfect hat

for him. The room filled with

cheers. Mr. Pockles looked

around. And laughed.

"Your turn, everyone!"

he declared. "Choose

your hats!"

And they did.

(Even the sun put his hat on.)

And so it was that Lady Fitz-Tulip got a beautiful new hat.

And Mr. Pockles went to Hat Day—with all of his hats at once.

But even better—with all of his new friends.

Just before they entered the PandaPolitan Club,

Lady Fitz-Tulip turned, raised her hat, and cheered.

"HATS OFF TO MR. POCKLES!"

Love

Tweedle

Zing

Dot

Sleepy
Time

Jungle
Safari

Sparrow

Lone
Star

Breakfast

Morris

Harvey